PRAYER DECLARATION SERIES

The Power is in Your Month

PRAYING

by the

BLOOD OF JESUS CHRIST

SARAH MORGAN

Copyright © 2018 SARAH MORGAN
All rights reserved.
ISBN: 978-1-7323220-0-4

Prayer Declaration Series
Praying By the Blood of Jesus Christ

Published by Morgan Publishing
P.O. Box 3701 Inglewood Ave. #134
Redondo Beach, CA 90278
1-888-320-5622 ext. 1

www.womenofvisionla.org
www.facebook.com/officialwomenofvisionla
www.twitter.com/womenofvisionla
www.periscope.com/womenofvisionla

ISBN: 978-1-7323220-0-4

Editing and typesetting by Fresh Reign Publishing

DEDICATION

I dedicate this series of books to the thousands of Prayer Academy Students across this nation, the Prayer Altar Call family, the intercessors at Vision International Ministries, and the countless elite warriors, intercessors, travailing women, and warring men. The Bible says, *The generous will prosper; those who refresh others will themselves be refreshed (Prov. 11:25 NIV).* As you have energized, restored, and revived others through your intercession, may you experience a wind of refreshing blowing over you in the place of PRAYER—the place of POWER!

Yours Truly,

Sarah Morgan
SARAH MORGAN

TABLE OF CONTENTS

PREFACE

HOW TO USE THIS BOOK

The Prayer Declaration Series is designed to strengthen your relationship with God by gaining an awareness of the importance of engaging in prayer for tangible results.

Effective prayer will cause you to soar like an eagle in God's plan for your life. It is a vital key to tapping into the wisdom of God, which will elevate you above mediocrity to produce astounding exploits to the Glory to God.

"...but the people who know their God shall prove themselves strong and shall stand firm and do exploits [for God]" (Daniel 11:32).

An intimate prayer life will stabilize and secure every area of your life. Contrary to some opinions, prayer should not be boring. Prayer should be the highlight of your day. Albeit, there is no set way to pray; there are guidelines:

1. Pray to God, the Father, in the name of Jesus Christ.
2. Seek to Establish a Good Personal Relationship with the Lord.
3. Make Sure Your Prayers Always Line Up With the Perfect Will of God for Your Life.
4. Back Up Your Prayers with Specific Scripture Verses.

5. Do not be Afraid to Write Your Prayers Out to the Lord.
6. Do not be Afraid to go into *Prevailing* Prayer, as Lead by the Holy Spirit.
7. Ask the Holy Spirit to Help You with Your Prayer Life (Romans 8:26).
8. Ask Others to Pray in Agreement with You When Needed.
9. Always Include Prayers of Thanksgiving.
10. Start with Early Morning Prayer and Keep an Ear Tuned to the Holy Spirit Throughout the Entire Day.
11. Read and use the Prayers/Confessions found in the Prayer Declaration Series.
12. Pray in the Holy Spirit. If You have Received the Gift of the Holy Spirit (the language of the Spirit), you can receive it today. If You Have not Received Him, ask; He will fill you. The Gift is Free!
13. Confess Scriptures Straight from the Word.
14. Pray a Scripture from the Word and Expand upon that Prayer, Spontaneously.
15. Pray the Word that is Hidden/Planted in your Heart, Spontaneously.
16. Receive Specific Guidance from the Holy Spirit as to What and How to Pray the Word.
17. Meditate on What You Read From Scripture and Pray the Word from Memory.
18. Pray God's Word and in Your Heavenly Language, and Alternate as the Spirit Leads.

Finally, have a great hunger for God—desperation to pray His will, and submit to Him from your heart/spirit. Allow the Holy Spirit to search you. Then, be diligent to crucify your flesh. Do not be satisfied with self-directed prayer; dig deep into the spirit realm.

When you allow the Holy Spirit to lead you, your spirit will issue, out the forces of life, in effectual fervent prayer. Continue to press into the spirit realm, until your spiritual antennas' tune in to the promptings and leadings of the Holy Spirit. Then as you speak every stronghold is destroyed, and the power of God released.

When you press into the place of prayer, in the spirit; your spirit becomes one with the Spirit of God. Then, you will pray His desires from your heart, and become intimate with Him, commune with Him, and become lost in Him. It is at that moment; your mind is in total subjection to pray the will of the Father.

Prayer is not forceful but flowing. Prayer is such a great joy that you cannot get enough. May the Spirit of Grace and Supplication fill you to overflowing in the *place of prayer*.

HOW TO ENTER INTO A TIME OF PRAYER

A.C.T

A - Acknowledge Him for Who He is.
Know ye that the LORD He is God: it is He that hath made us, and not we ourselves; we are His people, and the sheep of His pasture (Psalms 100:3).

C – Confess Your Sins, Faults and Shortcomings.
If we say that we have no sin, we deceive ourselves, and the truth is not in us. If we confess our sins, he is faithful and just to forgive us our sins, and to cleanse us from all unrighteousness (1 John 1:8-9).

T - Thanksgiving
Enter into his gates with thanksgiving, and into his courts with praise: be thankful unto him, and bless his name. (Psalms 100:4).

PRAYING BY THE BLOOD OF JESUS

The blood of Jesus is OUR Greatest Weapon of Victory!

And they overcame him by the blood of the Lamb, and by the word of their testimony; and they loved not their lives unto death (Revelations 12:11).

The blood of Jesus is our *weapon in prayer*; therefore our victory is sure.

SCRIPTURE REFERENCES

And the blood shall be to you for a token upon the houses where ye are: and when I see the blood, I will pass over you, and there shall no plague be upon you to destroy you, when I smite the land of Egypt (Exodus 12:13).

For the Lord will pass through to smite the Egyptians; and when he seeth the blood upon the lintel, and on the two side-posts, the Lord will pass over the door, and will not suffer the destroyer to come in unto your houses to smite you (Exodus 12:23).

For the life of the flesh is in the blood; and I have given it to you upon the altar to make atonement for your souls: for it is the blood that maketh an atonement for the soul. (Leviticus 17:11).

9

As for thee also, by the blood of thy covenant I have sent forth thy prisoners out of the pit wherein is no water (Zechariah 9:11).

For this is my blood of the new testament, which is shed for many for the remission of sins (Mathew 26:28).

Likewise also the cup after supper, saying, This cup is the new testament in my blood, which is shed for you (Luke 22:20).

Then, Jesus said unto them, Verily, verily, I say unto you, Except ye eat the flesh of the Son of man, and drink his blood, ye have no life in you (John 6:53).

Whoso eateth my flesh, and drinketh my blood, hath eternal life; and I will raise him up at the last day (John 6:54).

For my flesh is meat indeed, and my blood is drink indeed (John 6:55).

He that eateth my flesh, and drinketh my blood, dwelleth in me, and I in him (John 6:56).

In whom we have our redemption through his blood, the forgiveness of sins, according to the riches of his grace (Ephesians 1:7).

But now in Christ Jesus ye who sometimes were far off are made nigh by the blood of Christ (Ephesians 2:13).

And, having made peace through the blood of his cross, by him to reconcile all things unto himself; by him, I say, whether they be things in earth, or things in heaven (Colossians 1:20).

Forasmuch then as the children are partakers of flesh and blood, he also himself likewise took part of the same; that through death he might destroy him that had the power of death, that is, the devil; (Hebrews 2:14).

And almost all things are by the law purged with blood; and without shedding of blood is no remission (Hebrews 9:22).

But if we walk in the light, as He is in the light, we have fellowship one with another, and the blood of Jesus Christ His Son cleanses us from all sin (1 John 1:7).

And there are three that bear witness in earth: the Spirit, the water, and the blood; and these three agree in one (1 John 5:8).

But ye are come to Mount Zion, and to the city of the living God, the heavenly Jerusalem, and to an innumerable company of angels, To the general assembly and church of the firstborn, which are written in heaven, and to God the Judge of all, and

*to the spirits of just men made perfect, and to Jesus
the Mediator of the new covenant, and to the blood
of sprinkling that speaketh better things than that
of Abel (Hebrews 12:22-24).*

*Let us therefore come boldly unto the throne of
grace, that we may obtain mercy, and find grace
to help in time of need (Hebrews 4:16).*

*As for thee also, by the blood of thy covenant I have
sent forth thy prisoners out of the pit wherein is no
water. (Zechariah 9:11).*

DECLARATIONS

1. Thank You, Father, for the benefits and provision of the blood of Jesus.

2. I declare that I stand on the ground of the blood of Jesus to proclaim victory over satan and his agents and the world, in Jesus' name.

3. I plead and apply the blood of Jesus to every problem in my life, in Jesus' name.

4. I sprinkle the blood of Jesus upon my body from the top of my head to the soles of my feet.

5. I soak my life in the blood of Jesus.

6. I paralyze all satanic advancements delegated against me with the blood of Jesus.

7. I hold the blood of Jesus as a shield against any power that is assigned to resist me, in the name of Jesus.

8. By the blood of Jesus, I stand against every device of distraction.

9. I stand upon the Word of God, and I declare myself unmovable, in the name of Jesus.

10. I declare that every door that I have opened to the enemy be closed permanently with the blood of Jesus.

11. I decree and declare, by the tokens of the blood, by the voice of the blood, by the evidence speaking and the intercessions of the blood, that; through the shed blood of Jesus, I am redeemed out of the hand of the devil.

12. I walk in the light, and the blood of Jesus cleanses me from all sins.

13. Through the blood of Jesus, I am justified, sanctified and made holy with God's holiness.

14. Through the blood of Jesus, I have the life of God in me.

15. Through the blood of Jesus, I have access to the presence of the Lord.

16. Through the blood, I cancel every handwriting and ordinances written against me, my destiny and purpose, in Jesus' name.

17. I declare, by the blood, anything in me that is not of God is eradicated, in the mighty name of Jesus.

18. Let the blood of the Cross stand between me and any powers of darkness delegated against me, in Jesus' name.

19. I curse every work of darkness in my life to dry to the roots by the blood of Jesus.

20. I defeat, paralyze and erase, by the blood of Jesus, every spirit of
    - Demotion
    - Financial downgrading
    - Failure and defeat
    - Inherited problems
    - Vision killers
    - Dream attackers
    - Marital problems, in Jesus' name!

21. Let the power of the blood of Jesus be released on my behalf and let it speak against every dead bone in my life.

22. Let the power of the blood of Jesus be released on my behalf and let is speak against every INSURMOUNTABLE mountain in my life.

23. In the name of Jesus, I plead the blood of Jesus.

24. In the name of Jesus, I apply the blood of Jesus over my property, personage and children.

25. In the name of Jesus, I soak my ministry in the blood of Jesus.

26. In the name of Jesus, I apply the blood of Jesus over my business.

27. I draw a circle of the blood of Jesus around my city, region and neighborhood.

28. I draw the bloodline of protection around my community.

29. I overcome you satan by the blood of the Lamb.

30. You cannot put any sickness on me because the blood of the Lamb redeemed me.

31. Let the blood of Jesus speak confusion into the camp of the enemy.

32. Let the blood of Jesus speak destruction unto every diabolical growth in my life.

33. Let the blood of Jesus speak healing unto every infirmity in my life.

34. Let the blood of Jesus speak peace unto my chaos.

35. devil, by the blood of Jesus you are defeated.

36. The One who shed His blood and crushed your head; He is my Lord.

37. Let the blood of Jesus dry up tumors and growths.

38. Let the blood resist satanic projections and determinations, in Jesus' name.

39. Let the blood of Jesus break satanic networks and conspiracies, in Jesus' name.

40. Let the blood eradicate satanic verdicts, in Jesus' name.

41. Every generational verdict, I bring to bear the power of the blood of Jesus to bind you.

42. I render every evil power militating against me impotent by the blood of Jesus.

43. I hold the blood against you and declare that you are defeated.

44. Let the voice of the blood minister defeat to every evil determination in my life, in Jesus' name.

45. I superimpose the voice of the blood over and above every other voice, in Jesus' name.

46. By the voice of the blood, I decree death unto the enemy of the progress and advancement in my life in the name of Jesus.

47. By the voice of the blood, I break the cycle of negative events and bind the staying power of any problem in the name of Jesus.

48. By the voice of the blood, I create boundaries, borders and parameters against demonic assassins, in Jesus' name.

49. I decree that I am saturated in the blood, and when the enemy sees the blood, he will pass over.

50. Today, sickness and disease are passing over.

51. Today, poverty and lack are passing over.

52. Today, fear and timidity are passing over.

53. Today, frustration and harassment are passing over.

54. Today, satanic manipulations and intimidations are passing over.

55. Today, death and hell are passing over.

56. Today, by the tokens of the far superior blood of Jesus, I declare every curse is broken, in Jesus' name.

57. satan, the blood of Jesus is against you.

58. Today, I enter the holy of holies by the blood of Jesus.

59. Today, by the blood, I am exiting condemnation, and entering the realm of approval.

60. Today, by the blood, I am exiting debt and entering the realm of a clean credit status.

61. Today, by the blood, I am exiting delay and entering the realm of timeliness.

62. Today, by the blood, I am exiting denial and entering the realm of unrestricted access.

63. Today, by the blood, I am exiting discouragement and entering the realm of encouragement.

64. Today, by the blood, I am exiting distraction and entering the realm of focus.

65. Today, by the blood, I am exiting demotion and entering into the realm of promotion.

66. Today, by the blood, I am exiting lies and entering the realm of truth.

67. Today, by the blood, I am exiting hate and entering the realm of love.

68. Today, by the blood, I am exiting loneliness and entering the realm of comfort.

69. Today, by the blood, I am exiting emptiness and entering the realm of fulfillment.

70. Today, by the blood, I am exiting doubt and entering the realm of great faith.

71. Today, by the blood, I am exiting insecurity and entering into the realm of security.

72. Today, by the blood. I am exiting debt and entering into a realm of debt-free living and consistent cash flow.

73. Today, by the blood, I am exiting stagnation and entering the realm of unbroken momentum.

74. Today, the blood speaks redemption.

75. Today, the blood speaks justification.

76. Today, the blood speaks sanctification.

77. Today, the blood speaks my vindication.

78. Today, the blood speaks my compensation.

79. Today, the blood speaks my verification.

80. Today, the blood speaks my elevation and promotion.

81. I declare that the voice of the blood has silenced my accusers.

82. By the voice of the blood, today, every satanic accuser is silenced.

83. By the voice of the blood, today, every demonic accuser is silenced.

84. By the voice of the blood, today, every generational accuser is silenced.

85. By the voice of the blood, today, every ancestral accuser is silenced.

86. We overcome by the blood of the Lamb and by the word of our testimony.

87. I declare that by the blood of the Lamb I have overcome every obstacle; every test; every trial; every resistance and every challenge.

88. I declare that through the blood I am more than a conqueror in Christ Jesus.

89. I declare that through the blood I am victorious.

90. I declare that through the blood everything I touch shall prosper.

91. I declare that as long as the blood lives, as long as the blood speaks and the blood pleads our cause before the mercy seat; the blood will never lose its power.

92. By the tokens of the blood, I plead divine exemption and divine immunity for my family, friends and relatives; I declare no accidents or incidents; I declare no backlash or retaliation in the name of Jesus.

93. By the tokens of the blood, I issue a divine embargo against satanic attacks and permanent restraining orders against all demonic contenders.

I DECLARE THERE IS POWER IN THE BLOOD!

By the Covenant of the Blood...

I CANCEL... my name, the names of my children, friends, and relatives, from satanic altars, witchcraft covens and satanic registers, in Jesus' name.

By the Covenant of the Blood...

I CANCEL... the claims of premature death, untimely death and sudden death, in Jesus' name.

By the Covenant of the Blood...

I DECLARE... I shall not die but live, to declare the works of the Lord, in Jesus' name.

By the Covenant of the Blood...Like the woman with the issue of blood...

I CANCEL every blood issue in my life:
I CANCEL generational blood issues, in Jesus' name.
I CANCEL ancestral blood issues, in Jesus' name.
I CANCEL sexual blood issues, in Jesus' name.
I CANCEL covenantal blood issues, in Jesus' name.
I CANCEL soul tie blood issues, in Jesus' name.

By the Covenant of the Blood...

I DECLARE... my total emancipation from the pit of hopelessness, defeat, helplessness, denial and poverty, in Jesus' name.

By the Covenant of the Blood...

I DECLARE... my total emancipation from the pit of failure, shame and reproach, in Jesus' name.

By the Covenant of the Blood...

I DECLARE ... that I am propelled and transported into dimensions of miracles signs and wonders, in Jesus' name.

By the Covenant of the Blood...

I DECLARE ... that I am propelled and transported into dimensions of dominion, power and authority, in Jesus' name.

By the Covenant of the Blood...

I DECLARE... that I am propelled and transported into dimensions of the supernatural, in Jesus' name.

By the Covenant of the Blood...

I DECLARE... that I am propelled and transported into dimensions of Divine Revelation, in Jesus' name.

By the Covenant of the Blood...

Today, I activate into full motion and full power the activities, the interventions and the intercessions of the blood, in Jesus' name.

By the Covenant of the Blood...devil...hear me today...

I am soaked in the blood.
I am saturated in the blood.
I am covered in the blood.
I am drenched in the blood.

Therefore, I Decree and Declare by Reason of the Blood of Jesus...

I am untouchable!
unstoppable. In Jesus' name!!!

THE VOICE OF THE BLOOD

*As for you also, because of and for the sake of the
(covenant of the Lord with His people, which was
sealed with sprinkled) covenant blood, I have
released and sent forth your imprisoned people out
of the waterless pit (Zech 9:11 (AMP)*

By the Covenant of the Blood… I Declare My Total Emancipation…

From the pit of hopelessness.
From the pit of defeat.
From the pit of helplessness.
From the pit of denial.
From the pit of poverty.

I Declare My Total Emancipation From…

The pit of failure.
The pit of shame.
The pit of reproach.

By the Covenant of the Blood…

I am propelled into dimensions of the supernatural.
I am propelled into dimensions of miraculous signs
and wonders.
I am propelled into dimensions of dominion, power
and authority.

By the Covenant of the Blood...

I **COMMAND** my release from satanic covenants.
I **COMMAND** my release from satanic networks.
I **COMMAND** my release from satanic verdicts.
I **COMMAND** my release from satanic predictions.

By the Covenant of the Blood...

I **CANCEL** my name from satanic altars.
I **CANCEL** my name from witchcraft covens.
I **CANCEL** my name from satanic registers...
- Registers of premature death.
- Registers of untimely death.
- Registers of sudden death.
- Registers of witches and wizards, warlocks, sorcerers, enchanters.

By the Covenant of the Blood...

I **DECLARE** that no enchantment, no divination incensed against me shall stand.

By the Covenant of the Blood...

I **CANCEL** the claims of death.
I **CANCEL** the claims of hell.
I **CANCEL** the claims of the grave.

By the Covenant of the Blood…

I **DECLARE** I shall live.
I **DECLARE** my marriage shall live.
I **DECLARE** my business shall live.
I **DECLARE** my ministry shall live.
I **DECLARE** my children shall live.

I Demand a release. Let the Voice of the Blood…

Answer every accusation.
Answer every critic.
Answer cynic.

I Activate… into full power the activities of the blood and the intervention of the blood.

I Command the Voices that are Prevailing…

Against my breakthrough…
Against my miracles…
Against my destiny…
Against my finances to be silenced, by the voice of the blood of Jesus.

I Release into Full Motion…The Power of the Blood.

I speak my total release.
I speak my total deliverance.
I speak my total liberty and freedom.

I Declare I Am Coming Out by the Blood.

I am coming out of poverty.
I am coming out of bankruptcy.
I am coming out of foreclosure.
I am coming out of indebtedness.
I am coming out of health crisis.

My destiny is secure by the blood.
My future is secure by the blood.
My future is secure by the blood.

I Activate the Voice of the Blood... Against

satanic altars, deities, witchcraft powers, against spells and hexes, in Jesus' name.

I AM COMING OUT OF SATANIC IMPRISONMENTS!
I AM SOAKED IN THE BLOOD!
I AM SATURATED IN THE BLOOD!
I AM COVERED IN THE BLOOD!
I AM DRENCHED IN THE BLOOD!

I PLEAD the blood over my children, over my property and personage, in Jesus' name. Amen!

YOUR COVENANT COMMITMENT TO THE MINISTRY

1. PRAY daily for at least 15 minutes.
2. PRAY daily for divine protection for my family and me, as well as for our worldwide ministry team and their families, and our entire ministry.
3. PRAY daily for a harvest of souls around the world.
4. PRAY daily for your nation, its government, your church leaders, and for spiritual revival.
5. PRAY daily for the urgent prayer requests that come to the ministry from God's people around the globe.
6. PRAY daily for the other prayer warriors in this mighty army.
7. PRAISE God daily for the victories He is pouring upon the lives of His people.

OUR COVENANT COMMITMENT TO YOU

1. My team and I promise to pray daily for you and your loved ones.
2. You will be able to submit your prayer requests and praise reports directly to my private e-mail address explicitly reserved for members of the Prayer Academy, Elite Warriors.
3. We will stand in the gap on your behalf until you get the victory.
4. We will send you e-mails for special events that are occurring, as well as urgent prayer requests from people around the globe.

Prayer Declaration Series by Dr. Sarah Morgan

1. Activating and Affirming God's Prophecies and Promises
2. Affirmations of Faith
3. Blessed State of the Righteous
4. Breaking the Anti-Marriage Spirit
5. Breaking Dream Killers
6. Chain Breakers
7. Children's Prayers
8. Cleansing from Defilement
9. Destroying the Spirit of Stagnancy
10. Finances-Prosperity
11. Healing Prayer
12. Healing is for You
13. I Am Declarations
14. Praying by the Blood of Jesus
15. Prayers for Healing
16. Prayer for Husbands
17. Prophetic Call
18. Pursue and Overtake and Recover
19. Seven Mountain Prayer
20. Supernatural God
21. The Snare is Broken
22. Waiting on the Faithfulness and Loving Kindness of God
23. Weapons of Mass Destruction I
24. Weapons of Mass Destruction II
25. Wisdom

ADDITIONAL BOOKS BY DR. SARAH MORGAN

1. 7 Days of Fasting and Prayer
2. 21 Days of Fasting and Prayer
3. 30 Days of Fasting and Prayer
4. Confessing the Proverbs
5. Declaring the Psalms
6. Intercession by Pattern
7. Prayer the Master Key Revised Edition
8. Sing O' Barren Revised Edition
9. Seed of a Women
10. The Prayer Factor
11. The Faith Factor
12. You Shall Decree a Thing

To Sponsor a Prayer Academy Seminar in your city, to invite Dr. Sarah Morgan to your next conference, service, encounter, Revival, Crusade or for additional information, please contact the Prayer Academy Team.

Email: pastor@womenofvisionla.org
Phone: 1-888-320-5622 ext.1